# Showtime:

## Stage Fright

by

Leanne Van Dongen

RoseDog ❧ Books

PITTSBURGH, PENNSYLVANIA 15238

Dorrance Publishing Co
585 Alpha Drive
Pittsburgh, PA 15238
Visit our website at *www.dorrancebookstore.com*

ISBN: 978-1-6453-0515-6
eISBN: 978-1-6453-0497-5

Also by Leanne Van Dongen:

*Kate the Great*

*The Trio*

To my parents, for assisting with
the completion of my first book collection.

# SUNDAY

*Dear Diary,*

*Today, I'm going to achieve a goal I've been living up to: playing the piano on stage in front of a large audience. I've been waiting so long and now I'm going to do it. Other pianists will be there, too. I have to be honest though. I'm petrified. But Mom, Dad, Auntie Rebecca, Uncle Joseph, and my friends will be there watching, giving support. Having friends and family around always makes things better. I just don't want to mess up.*

Diaries are what you use to hide your deepest, darkest secrets. But I have one just to write about what's going to happen in my life or what has happened in the day, and I write in it every day.

I felt tapping on my knee and lifted my head from my diary to Mom's cheerful face. She mouthed something at me. I tugged one earbud out of my ear.

"What?"

"I said we're here."

My heart immediately thundered within my ribcage for two reasons: I'm petrified and excited. But mostly petrified. I turned the pop song off. (I'm a music lover. I love all types.)

I locked my diary and stuffed my hands into the pockets of my black dress to make sure the key was still there. It was.

As my parents exited the car, I wrapped my earphones around my iPod and went out of the car. I shut the door behind me and held my iPod out to Dad.

"Can you hang onto this for me?" I could have put it in my pocket, but anyone would be able to see the pocket sagging due to its weight.

Dad took it from me and put it in the pocket of his ripped jeans, and I could see the leopard print case through the tears.

I turned toward Hazel Grove Theatre. Auntie Rebecca, Uncle Joseph, and my friends, Valerie, Max, Daniel, Gavin, and Johnny were standing by the doors, waiting.

My parents and I made our way to them, and as we neared, Valerie saw us before everyone else. She wore a purple T-shirt, a denim skirt, and black sandals. Her long black hair had a tiny braid on the right side of her head. She took my hands in hers.

"You ready?"

"Yeah, but I'm so nervous." I turned to everyone else to see if they heard.

"You'll be fine," Daniel said as he placed his hand on my shoulder. *So he heard,* I thought. I wanted to believe him, but my anxiousness corrupted my trust in him.

He dropped his hand, and as he did, Uncle Joseph opened the double doors and we all walked into the busy theatre.

Gina, my piano teacher, was there, waiting for my arrival.

"Hannah, you're here."

I forced a smile. I should have been smiling automatically.

"Are you nervous?"

"Very."

She giggled. "Don't be. Come." She took my hand and led me down a hallway, my friends and family trailing behind. We came to a door and Gina pointed her crimson acrylic nail at it. "The auditorium's in there," she said to everyone behind us. And still holding my hand, she led me further down the hallway.

"Good luck, Hannah!" they called after me.

As we were turning, I looked back and grinned. We walked down a flight of stairs, my heart beating even faster. The stairs took us backstage and that was where all the other pianists were. (I noticed briefly that Hope glared at me, but I was too nervous to think about that.) The girls wore dresses like me and the boys just wore a nice shirt and pants. We're about the same age (twelve). The piano we were going to play was on the stage behind the closed dark blue curtains.

"The show begins in a couple minutes!" Gina announced to us.

I glanced around at the pianists; they didn't seem to be nervous at all. I guess I was the only one. And Gina knew that. She took my hands in hers. "Just breathe."

I tried to calm my heart by breathing in through my nose and out through my mouth.

"You don't even go on until everyone else has gone."

I nodded.

After a couple of minutes, the curtains opened, the spotlight shined down on the grand piano, a girl named Sarah went to it, and the audience applauded.

We all watched as she played soft music.

One by one, they played, and before Hope rose from the stool, she did something quickly, like fidgeting with something (at first, I didn't know what), and then she walked offstage. I thought it was a little strange, but whatever.

Then it was my turn.

"Remember."

I looked over my shoulder to Gina. "Just focus. No one is there. Only you. Good luck."

"Thank you." I tightened my ponytail and walked onstage and sat underneath the spotlight. I tried to ignore the applause the best I could, but I couldn't, and I felt more under pressure.

When the applause died away, I pressed down on the keys with shaky fingers and began playing. As I went on, my confidence grew. My mind was set on what I had to do and not fear. My nervousness disappeared little by little.

And then as I was halfway through playing the piece of music, a small figure crept into my peripheral vision. I glanced briskly at it and then looked back at the keys. And I immediately realized what I saw. My heart thundered as I looked again, straight into the eight eyes of a big, hairy spider, a tarantula.

I released a scream at the top of my lungs and sprung up from my seat. I backed away briskly and watched in absolute horror as it slowly stepped onto the keys.

I was breathing hard and kept watching it and turned to the murmuring crowd. They didn't know what was happening. I bolted off the stage and charged into Gina's arms.

"There's a tarantula on the piano!" I cried.

"What?"

I looked back at the spider. It was making its way across the keys. And though I was still terrified (I'm terrified of spiders), I grew furious. I had waited for this day to come, and when it arrived, it was robbed from me. All I'd wanted was to put on a wonderful show for my family and friends. And it was Hope's fault. She put it there to scare me because she and the other four people who bully me know what my major fear is.

As tears rained from my eyes, I fled from Gina's grasp and sprinted past the staring pianists, up the stairs, turned the corner, flew down the hallway into the lobby, and ran outside. I went to the side of the building and stood with my back against it. I breathed heavily and wept hard. Feeling as if I was about to collapse, I slid down the wall and tucked my legs in and hugged them.

And, unexpectedly, a semicircle of people formed in front of me.

Though I didn't want to meet anyone's eyes, I gazed up anyway- a horrible idea. I met the devilish eyes of Piper, her brother Ben, Willa, Stephanie, and Hope, who held the tarantula in her hands.

I stared at it in fear and they knew I was horrified.

"Great performance, Hanny," Piper "congratulated" me in her usual teasing, baby voice. She always did that to bother me. And it did.

Embarrassed, I stared down at my dress and said quietly, "Go away."

"You heard her. Go away."

Max, Gavin, Valerie, Daniel, and Johnny came up to us, and Max was the one who said that to them, and the one who looked angriest. He threw a finger at Hope. "And I feel like this is your fault. It looked like you put that tarantula on the piano to scare her." Max is my most protective friend. When people mess with his friends, he jumps in and saves them. In grades three and four, he was pretty violent, and when he got suspended after having to fight two guys at once (he took them on at the same time), he calmed down a bit.

Stephanie smirked. "It was just a little prank. Take it easy, Maxy."

Ben stepped in front of Hope and faced Max.

"Don't *ever* point your finger at her." He grabbed Max's finger.

We all watched them, and I was afraid of what was going to come out of this. But I practically already knew.

Max tensed and pulled out of Ben's grasp. "Don't *ever* touch me."

Ben smiled and stood face-to-face with him and tapped his nose.

And as if rage took control of Max, he threw himself at Ben and he tried to throw him to the ground, but Ben was resisting and fighting back.

We all watched them fight, worried.

When Max couldn't get Ben on the ground, he pushed him into the wall, a few feet away from me.

"Don't," I heard Valerie say. At first, I thought it was to stop the fight, but when I turned to her, she stood in front of me, facing Hope.

"But Mister wants to say hello to his new friend. What's wrong with that?"

I got up, my back still to the wall.

"Stop!"

Startled, we all turned to Uncle Joseph, who appeared ferocious, standing about ten feet away from us.

Hope backed away from me and Valerie, and Ben gave Max a final shove into the wall. But, of course, Max wouldn't have it and went to charge at Ben again, but Daniel put himself between them and put his hands on his shoulders, stopping Max from fighting Ben again when it had already ended.

Max accepted it and threw Daniel's hands off him.

And like scared animals, the bullies fled.

My friends and uncle turned to me.

"Are you okay?" Max asked, his curly, light brown hair messy from the fight.

Unable to speak, I simply nodded.

Uncle Joseph reached his hand out to me. "Come on, guys," he said to us, "we're done here."

I took his hand, and as a group, we walked back into the theatre to talk to Gina and my parents about everything that had happened before we all went home.

At home, I went to my room and slammed the door. I jumped onto my bed and buried my face in the pillow and sobbed all over again. What Hope did was stupid and immature, and because of the stunt she pulled off, she ruined my special moment. Gina told me that Hope would have to go find another teacher because she doesn't want a student like her. But that didn't fix anything. What's done is done.

# MONDAY

*Dear Diary,*

*I don't want to go to school because of THEM, and by "them," I mean Piper, Ben, Hope, Willa, and Stephanie. But now I'm just referring to them as "them." But my parents say I have to go. I'm scared and humiliated. I just want to stay home. I don't feel like facing my friends either. They saw what happened at the theatre yesterday. Hope put a tarantula on the piano and it scared me and I screamed in front of the entire crowd. I've never been so humiliated. What person would do that?*

"Hannah, time to go!" Mom called up the stairs. She sounded annoyed. Probably because I kept annoying her about wanting to stay home.

I put the lock on my diary and placed it and my pencil next to me on the bed. I reached down and picked up my neon pink and green backpack off the floor, swung my legs over the bedside, and put my bag on my back and went downstairs. I stomped all the way to the front door.

Dad was there, which he always is when I leave for school.

"Have a good day," he said as I tugged my pale pink flats onto my feet.

"How am I supposed to?" I grumbled, walking past him and through the door.

At the end of the driveway, I slowed down and stopped. I looked back to see if Dad or Mom were there watching from the door. They weren't. The door was closed.

I turned left toward Max's house, since we walk to school together every morning. I walked four houses down, and as I approached his big white house, I looked in through his bedroom window and glimpsed him walking by. There were no cars in the driveway, so Max was alone until I showed up.

I went to the door and knocked.

I normally hear the rush of footsteps as Max runs to the door, but that time I heard slow and faint stomping. Max answered in his dark blue housecoat and emoji pajama pants. His nose was red and his eyes were watering and his hair was all over the place. "Hey, Hannah."

"Are you sick?"

He nodded and sniffled and bent his head down as he sneezed. (I almost wished he sneezed on me.)

A horrible, sneaky thought popped into my head. "Can I come in?"

Max stared in confusion. "Why?"

I looked down at my shoes, unsure of how to respond.

"Is it because of Piper and those people?"

I tucked a long strand of brown hair behind my ear and nodded. I met his eyes. "Please let me in."

"I shouldn't."

"I know we could get in trouble, but as long as we keep it to ourselves, no one will know." I knew what I was asking of him was wrong and something I would never do, but I couldn't go to school. Not now. But I also thought of something else: if I didn't show up for class, my parents would get a call informing them I wasn't there. But I would explain the truth when the day was over.

Max sighed and stepped aside.

I stepped inside and he shut the door behind me. I stepped on the backs of my flats to get them off and tossed my backpack onto one of two couches.

"Do you want to play Minecraft?" Max asked.

"Yeah, sure."

We sat next to each other on the other couch in front of the TV. His Xbox One controllers were on the wooden coffee table between us and the TV and we each took one.

Max, Daniel, and I are huge Minecraft fans. Johnny and Gavin don't play it, and Valerie doesn't play video games, which, I think, is sad. Max and I like playing in survival mode since we think creative mode gets boring pretty fast, so we were playing in survival. We were standing in a cave lit up by lava. And then I heard a spider.

I turned around to see one charging at me. I hit it several times before it finally died. When I collected the string it dropped, a zombie appeared in the light of the lava. And more of them were approaching.

"We have to run," Max said. "There are too many." We ran a long distance before we were out of the cave and into the dark of the night on a mountain. The zombies were long gone.

Max put his feet on the coffee table, a toe peeking out of a hole in his sock.

"When do your parents come home?" I asked when the thought occurred.

"Dad comes at two and Mom comes home at two-thirty."

School ends at two-thirty, so I had a problem. "Okay, so what do-"

"Just hide in my room when my dad comes home," Max interrupted. "I'll come up with an excuse to get him to leave and then you can go home."

"Okay, cool."

We went back to our game and realized we were surrounded by monsters. "There's enough space between those two zombies for us two run through," I said. And we did just that, but then a skeleton fired an arrow at me, making me lose nine hit points.

We fled down the mountain, and when we made it to the bottom, we swam through a river to our house on the other side.

"When are you going to redo your performance?" Max asked all of a sudden.

I looked at him, not prepared for the question, but his eyes were glued to the TV. I didn't even think about redoing the performance. Honestly, I didn't want to do it again when I might be humiliated for the rest of my life. I didn't know how to answer him.

"Well...?"

"I don't think I'm going to," I admitted, turning back to the game.

As we went up to our rooms, Max asked, "What? Why?"

"I think I'm too humiliated. That happened in front of so many people."

We both went to bed and the screen dimmed, and in a matter of seconds, daylight filled our rooms.

"I understand. I think you're capable of another attempt, though." He appeared disappointed.

We turned to each other then and I said, "Everything was supposed to go right and Hope ruined it for me." My heart sank as flashbacks ran in circles in my head.

"You seem to be blaming yourself. It's not your fault it went wrong."

"Still."

"Try again."

"Too scared."

"Of what?"

I thought for a moment. "I think I might have stage fright."

"Seriously?"

I nodded, ashamed.

Max shook his head. Did he think I was being a baby?

"It happened *once.*"

"I've been on stage *once.*"

Max went silent and I continued. "That was my very first time going onstage and it was supposed to be perfect."

"You keep saying that. Why?"

It was my turn to fall silent.

"Do you feel as if you have to do everything right for your family and friends?"

I shrugged.

"We don't judge each other." He turned back to the TV, but my eyes were still stuck on him. "Talk to your parents," he basically ordered. "And Valerie. She's the best one to talk to." He sounded almost desperate for me to go again.

After two hours of Minecraft, we watched professional race car driving. (Totally not my thing, but Max wanted to watch it. I didn't enjoy race car driving because there were always way too many accidents.)

When an hour of misery passed, we ate cookies and drank iced tea while watching my favourite TV show. (Max hated Adventure Time more than I hated race car driving. It was payback.)

After three episodes, Max went upstairs to his room, abandoning me. He was done. But at least I didn't have to listen to him complaining anymore.

I watched four episodes before I turned the TV off and joined Max upstairs.

"I hate math," he groaned when I went to his side and eyed his homework.

"You and me both."

I watched him answer a question, and when he checked his answer and found out he got it wrong, he put his head down hard on the sheet.

"Do you need help?" I asked, though I already knew he needed a lot of it.

"You just said you hate math. That means you're bad at it, right?"

I pulled up another chair and sat with him at his desk. "I can try." I studied his notes a little and realized it was simple. I had learned this at the beginning of the year.

"Do you know what you're doing *now*?" I asked, irritated to the max.

"*No.*"

"Okay, I tried."

We heard a vehicle roll into the driveway. And we stared at each other. I walked to the window and looked out while trying to stay hidden at the same time.

"It's your dad."

"Okay, stay here. I'll try to make him leave so you can make your escape."

"Cool... What? It's not like we're spies."

"No, but I like to imagine that I am." His eyes widened and his face burned red more than his nose. "Forget I said that."

I laughed hard. "I'll hang onto that forever."

"Whatever. I'll just go."

As he went downstairs, the door screeched as it opened. "Hey, Max. Are you feeling any better?"

"Not really. Do you mind running to the store to get cough drops? My throat hurts."

"Sure."

I thought Mr. Lee was just about to leave, but then I heard, "Wait. Why did you need two plates and two glasses?"

My heart stung and then thundered.

"I... just felt like it," Max lied.

"And whose shoes are these?"

"Mom's."

"Her feet aren't that small. Whose backpack is that?"

"Mine?"

Silence.

"Is someone here?"

*Oh no.*

"Is someone here?!" Mr. Lee demanded.

"Hannah," Max confessed.

"Hannah!" Mr. Lee called.

Like terrible spies, we've been exposed; we didn't cover our tracks and Max came up with dumb lies not even a flamingo would believe.

I went downstairs and met Mr. Lee's furious eyes. In general, he's a good person and a great father to Max, but he's also strict, and when he's mad, he's terrifying.

When the unbearable lecture for me and Max ended, Mr. Lee drove me home. He wanted to discuss this with Mom.

"Mom!" I called.

She appeared at the top of the stairs. "Hey, how did school…" she saw Mr. Lee behind me… "go?"

"Hi, Bethany. Hannah's been at my house all day."

I felt super guilty.

Mom's eyes trailed back to me. "What?"

I said nothing and clutched the shoulder straps of my backpack.

"You didn't go to school?" Mom asked angrily.

"What did he just say?" I snapped, stepping on the backs of my flats and flung them angrily at the wall beside me. I marched up the stairs, past Mom, and went into my room and slammed the door. The force shook the house.

I lay down on my bed and listened to the intense chat between Mom and Max's dad. I knew I was going to be punished as soon as Mr. Lee left.

# TUESDAY

*Dear Diary,*

*I have so much to say. First, I skipped school yesterday and went to Max's house instead. He didn't go to school either because he was sick. His dad found out and told Mom and now we're both grounded. It was all my fault. I asked him to let me in and I knew it was bad. At least we got punished together. And second, I have to go to school, and I'll have a horrible morning. I have math first block with Hope and Willa. I'll try to survive, but we'll see.*

I locked my diary and went downstairs. I slid my feet into my poppy-decorated flats that matched my poppy-decorated dress. As I opened the door, I called, "Bye, Dad!"

"Bye!" he called from somewhere.

I closed the door behind me and miserably walked up the driveway and then walked along the side of the road.

"Hannah."

I turned and paused. Max was coming. But he was sick, so why was he coming.

"Are you coming to school?" I asked loud enough for him to hear from far away.

He nodded in reply, and I waited until he caught up before I started walking again.

"Why are you going to school?"

"I feel somewhat better." He sneezed.

"Sure you do."

We were quiet for a few seconds.

"I'm sorry I got you grounded."

"When my dad came back from taking you home, I told him I did it for you. That you got freaked out by-"

"Max!" I shrieked, turning to him. "Not everyone needs to know."

"Well, you didn't say that. And I told only *one* person. Anyway, it shortened my grounding."

I turned my attention back to the road, sighing. We crossed the street and turned left onto the sidewalk. Traffic zoomed by as Max said something, but I didn't hear. "What's that?"

"Did you talk to your parents and Valerie?"

"You're really pushing this," I remarked with a slight smile to hide my fear.

"Yes. Yes, I am."

"Do you want me to?"

"You should want to as well. People who care would say they want you to because we support you. Do you support yourself?"

Max had a point. He was supporting me, just like the rest of my friends and my family were. I should want to support myself, too.

We arrived at school and I went to my locker to get my math book. As I fidgeted with my lock, I heard Ben and Piper speaking to each other, and their voices grew louder as they neared me and they stopped behind me. I ignored Ben when he said, "Hi, Hanny. We missed you yesterday."

Feeling as if I was going to explode, I unzipped my backpack and put my book inside roughly. The hallways were the worst places to fight in (in my opinion) because other people would stop and watch and make unwanted comments.

"Come on, girl, talk to us," Piper said in her baby voice.

Still refusing to open my mouth, I shut my locker door and locked it. I put one arm through a shoulder strap and zigzagged through groups of students scattered around down the hallway to my math classroom. *They* were following close behind.

"Hanny," Piper whined. "You're hurting our feelings."

I felt insecure. But bullies do that; give you insecurity. That's all they do because they are the ones who are insecure. And they have nothing better to do with their lives. They target those they feel are too wimpy to speak up.

That was another reason I didn't want to go back on stage; I felt too insecure.

"Hanny," Ben mimics.

"Get lost." I tried not to react, but fury made me do it.

I didn't need to look to know they continued to follow me.

When I entered my classroom, I sat all the way at the other side of the room, and they stood in the doorway. They wouldn't leave.

I met my teacher's eyes.

"Good morning," Mr. Parker said with a smile. (He was the one teacher in the school who was always seen with a smile spread across his face.)

"Morning," I said, returning his smile, but there was no happiness behind it.

I could almost tell he sensed something was wrong because when the bell rang, Piper and Ben hadn't budged and he asked, "Can I help you?" He wasn't friendly anymore and he lost his smile.

They seemed startled. "Umm… no," Piper said shakily.

"Then go to class."

They gave me one last glare and took off.

Mr. Parker turned to me again with a concerned expression. "What's happening?"

I was debating an answer. When students began filling the class, I took lying into consideration. And when the guy whose desk I was sitting in stood next to me, I chose to lie. "It's all good." I stood up and apologized to the boy.

"It's cool" was his reply.

I walked to the other side of the classroom to where my desk was, feeling my teacher's eyes watching me go.

My desk was in the middle of two other desks, which was how the desks were arranged. I sat down in it and Gavin and

Daniel joined me at my sides. "What's up, Hannah?" Gavin said.

I shrugged and hung my backpack on the back of my chair, coming face-to-face with Hope. She leaned forward, her chin resting in her hands and her elbows on her desk. "Hi," she said innocently.

I turned back around.

Daniel noticed my frustration and looked back at Hope. "Quit it."

I didn't hear a word from her.

After a couple of minutes, the second bell rang and class began.

Mr. Parker stood before the class, a copy of the homework we had in hand.

"So, are there any questions regarding the homework?"

"Four and seven," Gavin called out.

The teacher began going through question four on the whiteboard when I felt something light hit the back of my head. I turned just in time to have a crumpled ball of paper hit my face. Hope and Willa were fighting back their giggles.

That was when it had gone too far. The bullying went from verbal to physical. I sprung up from my chair, sending it flying backwards, and faced my tormentors. The little wimp was gone.

"Listen!" I snapped, staring angrily down at them. "I didn't want any trouble. I haven't done anything wrong. You're both extremely immature and it's sickening. I don't deserve it. I come to school to learn, not to deal with you." I looked only at Hope then. "And ruining a show Gina put together for us the way you did was pathetic!"

I stormed out, tears springing to my eyes. It felt good to hold my own back for once, but I also just did that for the whole class to see. I felt humiliated all over again.

As my tears fell and feeling nauseas, I heard fast footsteps as if someone was coming after me. Ready for *them* to attack, I stopped short and whirled around; it was Daniel and Gavin. "You finally did something," Gavin said.

With my middle fingers, I wiped my tears away. "Yeah." I turned away and continued walking. "It was horrifying."

I actually felt something was going to erupt from within and I ran down the hall.

"Where are you going?" Daniel asked. He and Gavin were chasing after me, but I couldn't speak. I turned the corner and bolted halfway down the hall to the washroom. I went into a stall and the cereal I had this morning erupted out of my system. I heaved, feeling I wasn't done yet, and more rushed out.

Feeling I was finished, I stood up, flushed the vomit away, and went to the sink. I looked at my reflection. I was pale. I cupped water in my hands and rinsed out the disgusting taste in my mouth. At that moment, I felt as if everything was spiraling out of control for me. Nothing seemed to be going right anymore.

Outside the washroom, I found the boys waiting by the wall. They looked nervous. They must have heard me.

"You okay?" Daniel asked.

I took a deep breath, still catching my breath, and said fast, "Nothing's okay," and went back to the classroom. But before we walked in, I paused and turned to Gavin. "Can you get my stuff?"

He tilted his head. "Get your stuff?"

Annoyed, my eyes locked onto the wall across the hall and I repeated more firmly, "Can you get my stuff?"

"Okay, fine." I leaned against the wall closest to us and crossed my arms and I watched Gavin go into the classroom.

Daniel was about to go in, too, but he stopped and stared at me. "What are you going to do?"

I gazed at him for a moment and then looked down. I didn't want to answer. He took the hint and went in, and when Gavin returned, my eyes were still on the floor. "Here."

I looked up then and took my bag from him. "Is everything inside?"

"Yep."

"Thanks." I turned and left-literally left. I held myself together while I walked down the sidewalk, traffic around me.

I haven't been myself for two days now. I didn't know what was going on with me. Could nothing just go right?

At home, Dad was just about to leave for work. He opened his car door to get in but stopped when he saw me coming up to him. "What are you doing?" he asked, stunned.

"I need to talk to you," I said anxiously.

Dad glanced at his watch. "I'm running late."

"It's okay. I'll talk to Mom about it when she gets home. Is the door unlocked?"

He unlocked it and said, "I wish I could stay here with you, but my patient is getting heart surgery."

"Don't worry. I'm okay." I went in and shut the door.

Later that evening, I sat at my desk and gazed at the cotton candy sky through the window. Flashbacks of what happened this morning and what happened two days ago were still swirling around in my head, and no matter how hard I tried, I couldn't get them to leave me alone.

*Knock, knock* startled me. I heard the doorknob turning and the door widening. "How are you doing?" Mom asked in a gentle voice. I called Mom when Dad left for work. I didn't want to wait so long to talk to her about today.

My back was still to her when I replied, "Fine, I guess." I shrugged.

"Do you want to talk about it?"

"We already did."

"I think we should talk face-to-face." She sat on her knees beside me. "Look at me."

I breathed deeply and turned toward her. "First, Piper and Ben chased after me to Mr. Parker's room, and then when class started, Hope and Willa were throwing paper balls at me. I got triggered and yelled at them, in front of everyone, and I cried and went to the washroom, threw up, got Gavin to get my stuff for me, and I went home."

I thought Mom was going to remind me that I can't go to places far from the house alone, but she didn't.

"I called your school and told them you weren't feeling good and that you came home. They were a little disappointed that you left without notifying them, but they understood and signed you out. And I also spoke to the principal about the series of bullying that's been happening for some time now. He said that he would send an email to Piper's, Stephanie's, and those people's parents, saying it needs to end. Bullying is taken very seriously at your school."

"So it's over?"

Mom smiled and nodded.

I was in shock. I wasn't expecting to hear how the bullying had finally ended. Elated, I gave her a strong hug.

"I just wish you told me sooner," she said.

"I don't have an explanation for why I didn't." And then I thought of something else. Now that I was safe, I figured I could do this: I asked, "Can I have another go on stage?" with meaning.

Mom and I dropped our arms and held hands. "Do you want to?" Her smile still remained.

A smile stretched across my face when I nodded. Now that I didn't have to worry about being bullied anymore, I would try to move forward and never look back.

"I'll talk to Gina."

"Okay."

Mom kissed my forehead. "I'm so proud of you."

# WEDNESDAY

*Dear Diary,*

*Mom was right. The bullying is over and done with. Today at school, "they" completely avoided me. My friends noticed and Valerie wondered about it. I told them Mom sent an email to the principal explaining my situation. I told them Mom ended it all. She's taking me to the theatre right now. Yesterday, I told her I wanted another attempt on stage. She informed Gina and Gina booked the theatre for me to practice. Max kind of talked me into it, and I'm glad he did.*

Mom parked the car, and when I got out, the heat of the spring sun struck my face and exposed legs. I knew I should have worn a T-shirt. Instead I wore a furry long-sleeved shirt. Why?

I joined Mom on the other side of the car and muttered, "I hate the heat."

"I love it," Mom said, adjusting her sunglasses.

"I don't understand you," I joked.

Through the light brown lenses, I saw her roll her eyes playfully.

As we walked toward the building, Mom said, "I'm so proud of you."

"Yeah, you've been saying that a lot," I mentioned, eyes forward. "Max pretty much talked me into it."

"But *you're* the reason we're here now. Max was only guiding you."

We entered the theatre, but there was no sign of Gina. Mom gazed around for her. "She's not here."

*I can see that*, I thought. I leaned back against the window wall and Mom paced around.

Gina arrived shortly after we did and said, "Hi, Hannah."

"Hello."

The three of us went down to the stage. I sat down in front of the piano and looked at the keys. Was there venom on them? I was afraid to touch them.

"Whenever you're ready," Gina said from the front row.

"Is there venom or any diseases on it?" I asked with worry.

Mom and Gina chuckled. "No," they responded.

Feeling a little braver, I began playing... I looked up, expecting an enormous spider to fall from the ceiling and land on me. I pressed one key instead of the other. I sighed. Removing my hands from the keys, I turned to my mom and Gina. "Just relax," Mom soothed with a calming gesture of her hands.

"Nothing is going to happen," Gina added.

I glanced around the auditorium for *them*, but they weren't there. Why would they be? I was probably being dumb, but something still made me feel unsafe.

I played again, trying hard to focus and not freak out... another attempt failed. I dropped my hands at my sides and turned back to Mom at the sound of her voice. "You made it longer this time."

*Yeah. By three seconds.*

"Try again." There was a hint of frustration in her voice.

I shook my head. I felt pressured at that point, and as if Gina read the worriedness I must have shown on my face, she said, "She's scared, Bethany. It will take time for her to realize there's nothing to be afraid of. Hope's out and she's not coming back."

Mom sighed, but she got it.

Gina looked at me sympathetically. "Are you done for today?"

"Yes, please."

At seven, my homework was completed and I started the science project that was assigned today; we had to choose an ecosystem and describe ten animals that live in it and their way of surviving and create a presentation. I chose the Arctic ecosystem.

I researched how polar bears survive in a minus-forty environment.

Mom came up to me. "What are you doing?"

"Science project," I answered, eager to get on with it. I don't like being bothered when I'm working.

"How did it feel to be back on stage?"

"Horrifying." I was nervous to answer truthfully because I didn't want to disappoint her.

I scanned her face and quickly realized that was exactly what I did. "Horrifying?"

I nodded, heart sinking.

"Get over it. You're fine."

Eyes still locked, I became anxious again while Mom became frustrated. "I'm trying!" I shouted. "You should be proud of me for that! You were proud before! What happened?"

"I *am* proud. But I wish you would get over it and carry on."

My eyes narrowed and I shook my head. "What was that?"

Mom took a deep breath, like she was readying herself to say something, but nothing came. She left my room and shut the door hard. That was Mom's worst flaw; getting put off by things that she has no reason to get put off by. I noticed how she was getting put off at the theatre when I failed for the second time, well, third, and she basically ordered me to try again. It wasn't fair. Maybe I was being childish about it all, but when you're twelve years old (or any age as a kid), you can be scared for ridiculous reasons. Every child is going to handle frightening situations differently. Depending on the case, we could be traumatized longer than others, and that's okay. It's part of growing up. I wish Mom knew that. She still believes in me, just like Max. They both know that I have what it takes to overcome any obstacle that's stopping me from achieving any goal. It's just that sometimes I felt that Mom had a strict way of showing that she believed in me.

I knew I was going back up on that stage braver the next time. Not for Mom, not for Max, but for me.

Pushing my feelings aside, I went back to my project.


When I was tossing and turning for what felt like hours, I went downstairs to talk to Dad about Mom. I found him sitting on the couch, reading and drinking water with ice. "Hey, Dad?" I sat beside him.

He lay his book down on his lap. "Yeah?"

"I want to talk to you about something."

"Okay."

"Mom was a little mad earlier today because I was scared on the stage again today."

"Yeah, I know you feel like Mom can be too strict sometimes. I can perfectly understand how you feel because kids react to scary things differently."

"At least *someone* understands," I said dryly, sinking farther into the couch.

"I think she does understand, but she's strict. I can talk to her if you want. If it will make you feel better."

"Yeah, can you?"

"Of course."

I lightened up.

"Do you feel any pressure whatsoever?"

"A lot."

"Don't. Just do it for yourself."

I stood up and headed back to my room. "Night."

"Good night."

# THURSDAY

*Dear Diary,*

*I would have told you this before coming to school, but I was too busy listening to Dad and Mom debating about Mom being too hard on me, but anyways, I'm proud of myself for going back on that stage, but it was terrifying. Now I feel more pressured than scared. I almost want to give up. I feel very overwhelmed. I'm probably being a complete baby about it all. My life doesn't depend on playing the piano in front of an audience. There are other things I can do and still be happy.*

"Where's Johnny?" Valerie asked everyone at the table.

"Coming," Daniel answered.

"How did it go yesterday?" Gavin asked, and I knew exactly what he was talking about. "Pretty bad, honestly. I thought it would be better."

"What do you mean?" Max joined.

"So, I started playing, then I looked up at the ceiling thinking... something was going to fall on me-"

"A tarantula?" Gavin asked.

I nodded, sheepishly. "I thought a tarantula was going to fall on me, so I messed up, and I tried for the second time, and just… stopped."

"You're trying," Max remarked, biting into his chocolate chip cookie. "That's the main thing."

"It's too bad she doesn't see it that way," I mumbled but regretted it. I knew Mom understood. I looked down at my bracelet made up of tiny metal beads and music note charms.

"WHAT?!"

I jumped and met the shocked faces of my friends. I rested my cheek in my palm and laid out everything that happened between me and Mom. They listened to everything I had to say and they knew how I was feeling about it all.

"I don't think that was fair of your mom," Valerie remarked. "What you did was remarkable."

"My dad is pretty strict, too," Max added.

"I'm with Valerie," Johnny said as he sat beside her.

"I feel really stupid." I was looking at Johnny but was speaking to everyone. "That I'm scared of the whole tarantula thing. My piano teacher dealt with Hope, and I'm not being bullied anymore, so why should it happen again?"

"Exactly!" Valerie exclaimed.

We all stared at her and I felt hurt. I could see she regretted saying that. "I… didn't mean to be offensive."

"It's okay," I said strongly so she knew I was fine. But she still seemed guilty.

"Maybe you need us with you," Daniel said beside me. "We don't pressure each other. It can just be us."

I looked to everyone else and they all agreed. I gave a nod in appreciation.

That's the great thing with friends. You can always turn to them.

Soon, the bell rang and we went to our classes. I had French with Max. And I didn't like it. First, he was my only friend in the class, second, we sat with two other boys who were really good friends with him but not me (I rarely even talked to them), and third, a lot of students thought that Mme. Aguillard was too strict to be a middle school teacher. If someone did something that made her mad, she would give them detention without giving warnings first and gave them extra homework. She also assigned too much homework and wanted us to speak in French when talking to her, which we all had trouble doing at times. But she was good about it. Sometimes, and other students did this, too, I had to use my iPod to translate my question or answer in French so we could speak to her. (She let us use technology, which was reasonable.) The majority of her students were terrified of her, but I wasn't. I still got along with her really well and I wasn't a troublemaker. (Well, not usually.) The troublemakers were the ones who disliked her. (Max's two buddies. Whatever their names were.)

"You know," I started, "my life doesn't depend on-"

"Don't say it. You're going to make it happen."

We walked in and I followed him to the back corner to where his friends were, and when Max and I sat down, one asked him, "Did you finish the homework? Because we didn't."

Max was still as a rock until he slowly lowered his head down to his desk. "Nope."

I pulled hard on my binder to get it out of my gym gear. "I did it. You can copy if you want." I took out the worksheet and placed it in front of Max.

Max took his out and scribbled my answers down.

"Hey, girl."

I turned to Max's friend who sat right in front of me, startled. One just spoke to me. "Can we…?" He gestured to himself and the boy next to him and my work. I thought of saying no, but this was an opportunity for me to possibly get to talk to them more often. I didn't want to waste it. "Yeah."

They came over to our side and one stood beside Max and the other stood next to me and looked over my head to see my homework. I watched him copy it fast. But not fast enough. At the corner of my eye, Mme. Aguillard was coming. "Qu'est-ce faites-vous?" (What are you doing?)

We all turned to her, and I felt guilty right away. "Ils n'ont pas fini leurs devoir, alors je les aide," I already knew how to say. (They did not finish their homework, so I'm helping them.)

"En les laissant copier?" (By letting them copy?)

Other students in the class watched, and I felt embarrassed as I nodded. "Oui."

"Détention!"

We didn't talk much for the rest of class. But Max and I had gym next with Valerie, Johnny, Gavin, and Daniel, and it was the most fun class for all of us. The one class we had all together.

The bell rang and Max and I went down to the change rooms together. "I'm sorry for getting you in trouble," I said along the way there. "Again."

"It's okay."

It wasn't, and he knew it.

In the girls' change room, Valerie and I went into the stalls to change. I put on a purple T-shirt, black shorts with white stripes on the sides, and pink and orange sneakers.

I put my backpack in an empty locker and stood next to Valerie in front of the mirror as we put our hair up in ponytails. Then with the other girls in our class, we went into the gym. And as everyone in the class waited for Coach to show up, Max and I talked to our friends about French and detention.

"I had detention last week," Daniel said.

"For what?" Valerie asked.

He ran his hand through his blond hair before putting his hands in the pockets of his black and purple shorts and leaned back against the wall. "My brother and I-"

"Alright!" Coach interrupted. (His talking was more like yelling.) "Five laps around the gym!"

As a group, we all ran five laps of the gym.

He rolled a cart out from the equipment room and told us to line them up and then divide ourselves into two equal teams. We were playing dodgeball.

We lined them up and then divided ourselves as he said. My friends and I went to one side and others followed.

When we arranged ourselves, Coach studied the two teams. He pointed to the other side of the gym, saying, "This side needs more people! Max, go!"

"Can someone else-"

"Beat it, Max, you ain't one of us no more," Daniel demanded jokingly.

What Valerie and I loved most about gym was that Max, Gavin, Daniel, and Johnny insulted each other and they targeted one another in games.

Max grinned, finding Daniel amusing, and crossed the gym.

Coach blew the whistle and many people charged for the balls. (Some others and I were smart and stayed put because by going after the balls right away, you have a higher risk of being eliminated.)

A ball rolled toward me and I picked it up and charged at the girl closest to the center line. I chucked it at her and it bounced off her knee and she went off to the side.

Later into the game, it was only me, Daniel, and Gavin versus Max and two girls.

Max picked up a ball and aimed it at me. I was prepared to dodge whenever he released it. But he turned his aim to

Daniel and fired it, accidently getting him in the head. "Ahh!" Daniel shouted out with laughter as he went down.

"Man down!" Max shouted. He ran to our side to help Daniel to his feet. "You okay?" he asked, laughing.

"Yeah." He moved his hand from his head and revealed a red mark.

Coach called out, "Max, you're out!"

Max patted Daniel on the shoulder. "Sorry, bro."

"Oh, it's fine."


School ended. And Max and I went back to French for detention. His friends were already there and we joined them. Mme. Aguillard walked in and came over to us. "First," she started, in English, "homework always needs to be completed by its due date." Her glare was only for me, then, and I looked away. "And second, letting others copy your work is not acceptable." She went to her desk and returned with four worksheets. "Extra homework for you."

"Extra homework?" Max's friend shrieked.

Mme. Aguillard gave them to us and went back to her desk to get another sheet but different. She slammed it down on his desk. "And even more you, Oliver." *Oh, so that's his name,* I thought.

"WHAT?!"

"Maybe stop talking," Max's other friend suggested.

"Bye," she said sweetly to us.

We walked out, and outside the door, Oliver said to Max and the other guy, "Wow. That was rough."

"Oliver," I hissed, looking in the classroom. "She might hear-she heard you."

We all watched the teacher come. I was expecting something to happen to Oliver, but all the she did was reach for the door handle and began pulling. We stepped back to let the door come around and close.

Mme. Aguillard's final glare was for Oliver.

As a group, we walked down the hallway. "Well," Max started, looking passed me to Oliver, "she didn't get mad."

# FRIDAY

*Dear Diary,*

*My friends and I are on our way to the theatre. We agreed that it would be better if it was just us and no one else because we figured I would feel less pressured. I feel more confident in myself now that my great friends will be there watching me. I need their support to help me overcome my stage fright.*

Our bus came to a stop.

I put my diary in my backpack and followed my friends off the bus. (That was the first time I bussed with friends. I always went with my parents before.)

"The theatre is a block away," Max said, taking the lead. As the rest of us trailed behind, I said, "I really appreciate the support. Thank you."

"Yeah, you said that a hundred times," Daniel remarked from behind me. A smile was spreading across my face. (I tend to repeat the same things over and over. Like mother, like daughter.)

As the boys had their conversation, Valerie and I had ours. "So, how's your project coming along?" she asked.

"Good. How about yours?"

"Not that good."

"Why?"

"I can't decide on an ecosystem."

"So you haven't started," I remarked. We looked at each other and she shook her head. "I don't really like science," she said. "In general."

"I don't like it that much either."

"Like, depending on what we're learning, I like it, but other than that, I don't."

"Do you like it now?"

Valerie scrunched her face up. "Somewhat?"

We arrived at the theatre, and as they went to sit and watch me, I went on the stage, almost sure I could do this. Especially without Mom, though I felt bad for thinking of her that way. I was about to press down on a key, but my finger just stayed in the air above it.

"It's just us," Danial reminded me.

I gave him a weak smile and started to play. And as the soothing music filled my head, my anxiety drifted away. For the first time after my incident with the tarantula, I was at ease. My friends' presence was exactly what I needed the entire time.

"Hey, Hannah!" that voice I hated so much interrupted.

I was finally getting somewhere and *she* had to spoil it. Plus, wasn't the tormenting over? I slammed my fists down on the keys, making an ear-aching noise, and turned to *her*. My anxiety returned to haunt me forever.

"Get out," Valerie ordered as she stood up. The boys rose with her.

"Oh, calm down," Piper said. "I just came to say hello to Hannah." She said that as if she actually meant it. Which was totally not like her at all. And how did she know I was here?

"Hello. Good bye." Max waved her off.

With nothing else to say, Piper left. It was really strange.

My friends turned back to me, sadness in their eyes. "Again?" Gavin asked.

I breathed deeply. All of a sudden, I've had enough of being a wimp, and I've had enough of these stupid conversations about my stage fright. I began playing again and forced myself to focus on the soothing music travelling into my ears. Just like before, the fear went away and everything was okay.

At the end of the piece of music, I sighed with relief. I made it through. I turned to my friends, gleaming with pride.

After an hour of me playing and them being happy, we all went home. I walked in through the door and Dad asked from somewhere, "How was school and how did it go at the theatre?"

"Good."

"Mom told me you and three guys got detention in French yesterday."

"Why are we talking about this *now*?"

"Because she told me today."

"Shouldn't she have told you yesterday? The same day?"

"Whatever. Don't let people copy your work."

"I've been told already."

I went upstairs to work on my science project. That was all I had to do for the weekend.

With sheets scattered all over my desk, I worked on my PowerPoint, looking through every sheet of paper I wrote notes on… I wanted to quickly send an email to Gina. I wrote *Hi, Gina. I would like to redo the show if that's possible. It wasn't fair of Hope to ruin the show for me and the others. We all deserve another shot at it. Hannah Little.* I sent it off and continued reading through my notes and putting them in my presentation.

I was half-way through the project when I got a notification from my email. Gina replied with *Hi, Hannah. I'll try to arrange another show, but I have to talk to different people, so it might take some time. Good on you for wanting to do this. And I think the other pianists would want another show since theirs was also ruined. You're a star. Sincerely, Gina.*

I was very excited. "Mom! Dad!"

They both came running as if something was wrong. "Gina said that she'll try to arrange another show."

Mom grinned. "That's great."

"I emailed her."

Mom and Dad stared. "You did?" they asked at the same time.

"Yeah. I want another go at it."

Mom wrapped her arms around me. "That's awesome."

Dad patted me on the head.

I was looking forward to it, if it was even going to happen, but I knew that I was going to need more practice. I managed to play once without stopping. I have to be able to do that again and again.

# SATURDAY

*Dear Diary,*

*Today, Valerie and I are going back to the theatre. Gina may arrange another show for me and the other pianists, so I think it would be a good idea if I practiced getting used to being back on stage. It went really well yesterday. I have to be able to do it over and over.*

As I had iced tea, I worked on my project.

And I did that for an hour because Valerie came to my door.

"Hi," she said when I answered it. Her dress caught my attention. It was a light blue choker with one-quarter sleeves and had glittery black-and-silver flowers all over it. I don't care for dresses that much. I prefer shirts and skirts. Like what I wore now; a plain white T-shirt and a black denim skirt with buttons going up the front. And my charm bracelet. "I like your dress," I said.

"Thanks."

I put my sandals on and we followed Mom into the jeep. She drove us to the theatre.

"How long are you going to be?" she asked when she pulled up in front of the building.

"About an hour?" Valerie answered for me.

"Okay, I'll just go to the library."

"Okay," I said and followed my friend into the theatre. In the lobby, she stopped to let me take the lead. I led her to the door of the auditorium and I asked, "Do you maybe want to hang out after this?"

"Sure. At your place or mine? I think it would be better if we went to yours because my mom is cleaning the house."

"Okay, sure."

Valerie went through the door and I went down the hallway, turned the corner, and went down the flight of stairs to the stage, fearless. Then I sat on the stool in front of the grand piano.

"Just remember that it's only us," Valerie calmly said from the front row.

"I know," I said, looking at the piano. And I played, my heart thumping lightly.

And it was when the music died that I realized I was making it and made it through. Another success.

Valerie clapped. "That was beautiful," she complimented.

I played again and again until I heard the door open and I knew who it was. I stopped halfway through the song and Mom walked down the stairs to stand next to Valerie.

"Why'd you stop?" Valerie asked sadly. "You were doing excellent."

I didn't know what to say. "...I'm just done now." I decided to change the subject before Valerie had time to object. "Can Valerie come over, Mom?"

"Of course." Mom gave her phone to Valerie so she could call her mom for permission to come over.

We went into my room and I said, "I'm almost done with the project."

"I've barely started."

"Seriously?"

Valerie closed her eyes and nodded.

"It's due on Wednesday." I was concerned.

"Yeah, I know."

I sat down at my desk and turned my laptop on, Valerie standing beside me with an arm around my shoulders. I opened my PowerPoint... and I didn't save the work I did earlier and it was gone.

"Are you kidding me?" I shrieked.

"What's the problem?"

"I didn't save the work I've done today. I have to do it again." (I'm one of those people who hate redoing things that take a lot of time and effort. Except doing the show for the second time.)

"It's okay. Just do it again."

*Like I have a choice.*

"Just be glad you're not in *my* position. Valerie removed

her arm from my shoulders and lay down on my bed, propped up on an elbow.

I closed my laptop and turned in my swivel chair to face her. "Why haven't you started?"

"I started but haven't done much."

"What have you done?"

"I figured out what ecosystem to do."

"That's it?"

"Disappointing, I know."

"What ecosystem?"

"Arctic."

"Same."

Suddenly feeling hot, I slid the window open to welcome the cool breeze into the room. "You know," I started, thinking of another topic to talk about. "I've been in trouble quite a bit lately."

"Have you?"

I fidgeted with the music note charms on my bracelet as I recalled the first day it began. "Well, there was the disaster on Sunday-"

"Oh, yeah."

"-and then on Monday, I skipped school and went to Max's house instead. I was too embarrassed to go-"

"I get that."

"-and Max's dad found out that I was there during school hours and then he told my mom and Max and I got grounded."

"For how long?"

"For me, three days. For Max, no idea. Anyways, I *never* skipped school before. And then on Thursday, I let Max and his two friends copy my French homework-"

"And you all got detention," Valerie finished for me. "But you know what, though?"

We looked at each other hard in the eyes. "You've been bullied for a long time. That can make you do things you wouldn't normally, or ever, do. Bullies can put you in the wrong state of mind. You're *not* someone who skips school-"

"I am *now*."

Valerie shook her head. "And you *don't* let people copy your work."

"I do *now*."

"Stop it. You're not that kind of person. And I think that for a while, you won't be yourself. You're still recovering from a series of teasing. You feel lost, and that's okay. You'll find yourself again. You already are finding yourself."

I gave her a slight smile and lost eye contact, eyes now on her dress.

"You're okay, and getting back on that stage couldn't have been easy. But you did it because you're not a quitter and you're strong. You're not letting the bad memories break you anymore."

I met her dark eyes again. "Thanks." We stood up at the same time and held each other.

I'm glad to have a friend like Valerie. I know I can always turn to her when I need someone.

"Do you want to go to the park?" I asked.

"I'm in a dress."

I lent her a tank top and shorts.

We turned left toward Max's house and kept going. Across the street was a fenced-in field with a playground in the center.

The entrance was all the way at the other side, so we climbed the fence and jumped over, landing on our feet with a *thud*.

About six kids, maybe a bit older than us, were playing soccer, and when we were going to the swings, one noticed us and asked, "Hey, do you guys want to play?"

Valerie and I turned to each other and then back at the boy who asked. I thought it would be cool to be hanging out with teenagers. My friends and I never did that in school. "Sure," I said.

After introductions, Valerie and I were separated between the two teams

The guy who invited us to play passed me the ball, and I ran with it. When I couldn't get past two people blocking my way (Valerie being one), I kicked it to Samantha (a girl on my team). She became the new target. My path was no longer blocked and I ran as fast as my feet could take me to the other end of the field.

She still had the ball, making her way to the goalposts. "Pass!" I shouted.

She saw me and kicked it hard, making it soar through the air and landing at my feet. I turned to the goalie, who was ready to block my shot.

I aimed for a corner and pulled my foot back, pretend-ing to send the ball flying in that direction to confuse the goalie, but I quickly changed position and sent it flying to the other corner.

Ben (another Ben) realized I tricked him and tried to catch the ball heading into the corner I was really aiming at. But he didn't make it in time. The ball went in.

I was having fun playing soccer with a group of six teens. And I could tell by how Valerie was panting and sweating and smiling that she was loving it.

When the sky was pinking, we called it the day. Valerie's team won six to four, but I still had tons of fun.

"You guys should play with us more often," Valerie's team-mate Matt said to me and Valerie. "We come out every Saturday."

"Yeah, okay," Valerie said, breathing hard. "Sounds good."

They high-fived us and we all went home.

As I was walking back to my house, I thought about how cool it was to be playing soccer at a park with kids a few years older than us. I was used to being around kids the exact age as me. I definitely wanted to do that again with Valerie.

# SUNDAY

*Dear Diary,*

*I'm seriously debating whether to practice alone or have Mom there with me. I haven't been giving it much thought, but I'm still a little upset about how she's been acting about my stage fright when I had it. But I know she didn't mean bad. She's just a little strict, like a lot of parents are. I think she should know how much I've improved. It would make her so happy to see how well I'm doing. I'm just worried if I feel pressured by her, my stage fright will come back, and I'll have to work hard to get rid of it again. But I think I'll take the risk. I can just tell her to go easy on me. Children have to be able to speak to their parents if something is troubling them. Okay, I'll discuss it with her.*

*Knock, knock.*

I whirled around in my swivel chair to see Mom entering. "Are you ready to go?"

"…Yes…but I want to talk to you about something."

She smiled and crouched down in front of me.

"I feel like that since you're my mother, I can talk to you about anything."

"Absolutely." She smiled sweetly.

I started to lose the strength to keep hold of her eyes. But I quickly regained it. "Sometimes I feel like you're too hard on me."

Mom lost her smile.

"I don't have stage fright anymore and I don't want it back, but at the same time, I want you to watch me so you can see how much I've improved. But I'm not sure if that's a good idea. I'm just worried that if you're there, I'll get my stage fright back. Then I'll have to get rid of it all over again." I was fearful to see what her reaction would be.

"In what way do you feel as if I'm hard on you?" she asked calmly.

"When I can't do something right, you get frustrated. Like, I told myself before the show, I can't mess up. I often feel like I have to be perfect for you. Do I?" I had an urge to break down, but I held it together.

Mom tilted her head, eyeing my face. "No, honey. Of course you don't have to be perfect. I know I can be like that, and I'll be easier on you. But you need to know that a lot of parents are going to be a little strict. I never meant to make you upset."

We were both silent until she placed her hands atop my knees and continued with, "Dad and I had this discussion already."

"I know, but I think it should be coming from me."

"It should. Can I please watch you play?" She puppy-faced me.

I smiled. "Okay."

We hugged and Mom said so quietly, I barely heard, "I'm sorry."

"It's okay."

"Let's go."

We went in the jeep, and as we drove, I told her, "Valerie and I were talking about Piper, Ben, and the others and Valerie said that bullies can put you in the wrong state of mind."

Mom nodded in agreement. "It's true. They can mess with your mentality."

"Do you think that was why I was paranoid about giant spiders raining down on me?"

"Could be." Mom shrugged.

I stared at her, waiting for more.

"Being taunted can *really* take quite an effect on you. Some cases are worse than others, and it usually starts with a little teasing to the point where it's almost out of control. It had to stop before it got worse."

"It was so bad that I don't think it could have gotten worse."

"Trust me. It could have."

I considered everything she said. "How do you know so much about this?"

Mom didn't answer.

"Tell me."

Mom sighed. "I went through quite a bit of bullying in school. It started with a little teasing and then it turned to name-calling and then they went after my friends. We thought we could handle it ourselves… It only escalated. And then we saw a school counsellor."

"They called me 'Hanny,'" I told her.

"Yeah, I was called immature things, too. It didn't hurt my feelings, but it was annoying. My name is Bethany and I want to be called *Bethany*."

"It didn't hurt my feelings either. I just want to be called by my real name, too."


At the theatre, I played classical piano music for Mom and she loved it. And I felt no insecurity from her. I played once.

Twice.

Three times. Each time more fluent than the one before.

"Beautiful!" Mom exclaimed. "You're amazing!"

I felt myself glowing.

During the fourth time, I pressed down on the wrong key, and I felt some kind of pinching inside. I turned to Mom. "Don't worry. You can do it."

So I did it again, and succeeded again.

"Well done."

But it wasn't Mom's voice.

I turned to see Dad seated with Mom.

I played over and over for probably an hour. I really wasn't keeping track.

And when I figured it was time to stop, I stood up from the stool. "I'm done now."

"Should we go out for lunch?" Dad asked.

"Alright."

"Sure," Mom seconded.

I rode with Dad.

"You really are extraordinary," Dad said with a wide grin stretching from cheek to cheek. "You know that, right?"

"Yeah, I know," I replied jokingly. (Though I kind of meant it.)


As I ate pancakes drenched in syrup, I told Mom and Dad how Valerie and I played soccer with a bunch of teenagers.

"*That* must have been neat," Dad remarked.

"It was. And Matt, one of them, said that we should come out more often."

I turned to Mom. She had a slight frown on her face.

"Is that a bad thing?" I asked.

"It's not a bad thing, but I think you're a little too young to be playing soccer with kids older than you."

"What's the problem with that?" Dad asked. "It's not like she'll be hanging out with them all the time." Dad paused and turned to me.

"They said they come out on Saturdays, but that doesn't mean I have to be there every Saturday."

"Then it's okay," Mom said. "Sorry, I'm just used to you being around Max, Valerie, and those people."

"I think it's nice they offered you and Valerie to play with them," Dad said.

"It was a lot of fun, and Valerie really liked it."

# MONDAY

*Dear Diary,*

*After having a good conversation with Mom, I let her watch me play. It felt good to have a peaceful word with her. I kept my emotions bundled up inside for too long. It was such a relief to let them out. And Mom and Dad were happy to see that I haven't given up.*

"Hannah, we have to go!" Dad called.

I grabbed my backpack and ran outside to his convertible. He was already sitting at the wheel when I hopped in beside him.

Dad pulled out of the driveway and onto the street, the spring wind blowing through my ponytail.

"What classes do you have today?"

"Science, socials, English, then computers."

"Nice."

I went to my science class and sat next to Gavin, the only friend I had in the class. "So," I started, "I went to the theatre yesterday and my mom watched."

Gavin's green eyes widened. "Oh, good. Were you okay?"

"I was fine. Before we went, though, I talked to her about her being too hard on me. I told her how I felt about it, and it was all good."

"It was good you explained yourself to your mom. Kids have to be able to talk to their parents if something is bugging them."

"Yeah, exactly."

"I'm glad it all went well."

I nodded my thanks.

The second bell rang and Ms. Alcoser walked in and sat at the front of the room. "How was everyone's weekend?" she asked in her Mexican Spanish accent. (She was a new teacher at Hazel Grove Middle School.) She asked this every week.

Some people said "good" and others actually talked about their weekends, but I said nothing. I never really talk about my weekends with teachers. Unless they ask me directly. It was the same with Gavin. We're both a little shy.

After story time, Ms. Alcoser said, "I just want to remind you that your presentations are on Wednesday. I'm giving you this block to work on them."

I was stunned. "Seriously?" I whispered to myself, but Gavin overheard. "What?"

I was partially listening to the teacher when I silently said, "I finished it this weekend. I could have had it off. What am I supposed to do?"

So for the duration of class, I just had random conversations with Gavin while he worked on his project: Minecraft, his baseball game on Saturday, ice cream, and Johnny's crazy party back in January.

Then finally the bell rang.

I went to social studies.

The desks were arranged with two or three desks put together and faced the front. Where I sat, there were three desks in a row and I sat on one end, Valerie on the other, and Daniel in the middle.

He was there when I sat down. "Hey," he said. But he wasn't looking at me. He had his eyes down on his phone.

"Hey," I said back.

And then Valerie walked in and sat down on the other side of him.

For the entire class, we talked about current events, which I thought was extremely boring.

The rest of the day was better. In English, we had to read a short story and had to write a part two of it. I like writing stories, so it was fun. And what I liked about English was that Mrs. Schwarz never gave us homework. Everything was done in class, and if we didn't finish assignments during class, she would give us the next day to. Also, the work was pretty easy, I thought.

And my last class was computers. My favourite class. I had two friends in it, but they weren't the ones I hung out with the most. They were Jennifer (Jen) and Madilyn (Maddie).

I sat in front of the computer and Maddie was the first to notice me. "Hello." Her voice was soft and gentle. She's a really shy and quiet person. And fashionable. She always went to school dressed really nicely. She wore a tie dye T-shirt under a ripped jean vest, a pink flowy skirt, white flats, a ring, and a white ribbon in her dark brown hair. (She had an obsession with wearing a ribbon in her hair.) And her nails were pink and sparkly.

"Hi," I said to both girls, and it was Jen's turn to notice me. "Hey," she said to me.

She dressed more casually; a pink and purple sunset-like shirt, grey jean shorts, and black sandals. Her strawberry blonde hair was in a bun.

When the teacher explained the next assignment, we all got to work. And, as always, chatter filled the room.

As Jen, Maddie, and I worked, we had our own conversation that lasted the entire block.

School ended and Maddie and I went down the hallway together. We got picked up at the same place each day. But we waited until we were outside to talk since the hallway was a zoo.

At the fence, I asked, "So, how was your day?"

Maddie shrugged. "Boring."

"The first half of my day was really boring."
We didn't talk for long. Dad honked and I said, "See ya."
Maddie only waved.

# TUESDAY

*Dear Diary,*

*The show is happening this Friday! I'm really excited, but petrified. Just like before. I'm on my way to the theatre right now. Auntie Rebecca and Uncle Joseph picked me up from school today to watch me. I told them the show is this Friday, and they said they'll be there. I also told my friends the exciting news today, and they're going to try to make it.*

With rock music playing loudly in my ears, I looked out the truck window at the theatre as we came to a stop in the parking lot. I tugged my earbuds out and wrapped them around my iPod and tucked it away in my bag. I exited the truck and waited for my aunt and uncle to finish their conversation. I examined Uncle Joseph's truck; it was black with red-and-orange flames on the sides. He's really interested in art and painting and he's skillful. He spray painted the flames himself. He also spray painted Auntie Rebecca's car, a silver mustang with black-and-blue angel wings on the hood. It looks really pretty. But he makes his living on woodwork.

When they were ready, we all walked into the theatre. Auntie Rebecca and Uncle Joseph went to go sit and I went to the piano. But before I played, I glanced at them to see if they were ready. Their eyes were on me and Uncle Joseph nodded, telling me they were.

So I filled the auditorium with peaceful music, and that time, it sounded more peaceful than it did the last time. Probably because I've been hearing it over and over again and it was sounding more fluent.

When the music came to an end, I received an applause. I knew I was prepared for the performance. But if I stopped practicing, I might have lost it, so I had to keep it up. But practicing this much was beginning to get tiresome.

After I'd gone through it twice more, we went to a nearby bakery for ice cream.

I saved a table by the window while my aunt and uncle got the ice cream. I gazed out the window, watching traffic zoom by. (Hazel Grove is a very busy community, if you haven't noticed yet.)

Auntie Rebecca placed vanilla ice cream in a cup in front of me. "Thanks," I said.

She sat beside me and Uncle Joseph sat in front of her. He asked, "How was school?"

"Good. I had French, gym, math, and sewing."

"Sewing was my favourite class in high school," said my aunt.

"I would think so," I said, raising my eyebrows. "You *are* working toward being a fashion designer. I think you'll get there."

Auntie Rebecca beamed. "Thanks, missy."

And I meant it. I saw the gowns she made and they were really detailed and gorgeous.

"What are you doing in sewing class?" my aunt asked.

"We're sewing stuffed animals. It's kind of difficult. I'm making a dog and I tried to make the ears the same size only to have one bigger than the other." I took sewing class seriously and got upset when I messed up, but we just learned to make animals last week, so I guess it wasn't fair to be upset with myself.

"Yeah, animals are complicated," Auntie Rebecca agreed. "I prefer dresses and skirts."

"Of course you do."

She beamed again.

"What did you do in your other classes?" my uncle asked.

"In French, we started learning about family members and did a worksheet. In gym, we played ball hockey. It was fun. I got a goal. And in math, we just did textbook work."

"How's math this year? Because I know you had issues with it last year."

"It's going way better. I have a better teacher this year and math actually makes sense now. Even when I had a tutor it was hard."

"What's your favourite class?" Uncle Joseph asked, putting a spoonful of chocolate ice cream in his mouth. That reminded me that I hadn't even touched mine. I put a spoonful in my mouth, which wasn't the smartest idea because the ice cream touched my tooth and it ached. I had my mouth open to let it melt before I swallowed. "Cold," I tried to say but couldn't form the word. My aunt and uncle were looking.

After a moment, I was able to swallow, and I chuckled with them. "Computers," I finally answered.

"Oh, yeah?"

I nodded.

"That was one of mine. My other favourite was wood-work."

My face turned sour. "I didn't enjoy it at all."

"You took it?"

"It was in the rotation last year. It was too hard for me. My birdhouse was a disaster."

He snickered.

"What did *you* make," Auntie Rebecca asked him.

He threw himself back in his chair, cocked his head, and stared at her gloomily.

I laughed.

"You know what I made."

I looked at my aunt then. She was confused.

"The birdhouse hanging from the roof over the deck."

"Oh, yeah."

*"Oh, yeah,"* he mocked playfully in a sarcastic deep voice. I smiled before revealing teeth.

He turned his attention to me. "You know, I have a day off on Thursday. Maybe I can pick you up from school, take you back to our place, and we can build a birdhouse."

As exciting as that would be, I remembered how wood-work went for me. But Uncle Joseph makes everything fun, so I nodded.

"Do you like your teachers?" Uncle Joseph asked.

"The majority of them. One is too strict to be a middle school teacher. Maybe even too strict for high school."

"What's her name?" Auntie Rebecca asked.

"Mme. Aguillard."

"French teacher?" my uncle asked.

"Yep."

"Who would you say is one of your favourites?" my aunt asked.

I thought hard for a moment. "Probably Mrs. Schwarz. Her work is really easy and she doesn't give homework. The one teacher of mine who doesn't."

"That's nice," Uncle Joseph said and I nodded.

"Too much homework is overwhelming," I said.

"I remember one teacher I had; she gave us a lot of home-work every class. I hated it."

"I'm sure the rest of the class did, too," I agreed.

# WEDNESDAY

*Dear Diary,*

*I actually don't have anything to say today. Except that I'm presenting my science project to the class.*

I locked my diary and got dressed. I put on a lime green T-shirt with white varsity stripes, a denim skirt with a flower on one of the back pockets, a belt, and a necklace. I put my hair in a ponytail that went over my shoulder.

I went to the bathroom to brush my teeth, back to my bedroom to get my backpack, and then went downstairs to put my sandals on. "Mom, are you ready?" I asked loudly. It really should have been her asking me.

"Yep!" her voice called. "Coming!"

My first class was social studies, and we did current events. Again.

"We do this way too often," I overheard Daniel whispering to Valerie.

"I know. I'm so bored," she whispered back.

I agreed with both of them; after doing it for so long, I thought it was time to move on.

I glanced around the room to see if anyone else was bored.

So social studies went by not fast enough and science was my next class. I knew it was going to be better.

After the second bell rang, Ms. Alcoser asked, "Who's presenting first?"

I raised my hand. I always want to be the first to present.

She saw me. "Sure, Hannah."

I took my laptop out of my bag and walked to the front. I connected it to the projector and "ARCTIC ECOSYSTEM" appeared in a snowy environment on the whiteboard.

I turned the lights off and my presentation began. "Arctic ecosystem," I began. I went to the next slide on polar bears. "Polar bears have extremely thick fur that warms their bodies in a minus-forty environment. Their fur is so thick that they can swim in icy water without feeling a touch of coldness. Polar bears eat a variety of things, such as seals, young walruses, reindeer, small rodents, seabirds, waterfowl, fish, and berries."

Next slide: "Seals have a thick layer of blubber, or fat, to keep their organs insulated. Younger seals are kept warm by a layer of water-repellent fur. Seals eat things like squid, crustaceans, and variations of fish."

Throughout my presentation, I occasionally made eye contact with the class, even though it was intimidating. And it was even worse when I explained the diagram of the snowy owl.

At the end of my presentation, everyone clapped and I disconnected my laptop from the projector.

"That was good," Ms. Alcoser complimented. She turned to the class. "Who's next?"

Gavin lifted his hand, surprisingly. He was usually one of the last few people to present. He didn't like presenting. But I guess I inspired him to just go and be done with it.

I sat down beside him and watched as he took the rubber band off his poster and it unraveled. He carried it with both hands to the front and placed it under the overhead. His aquatic poster appeared on the board.

"I chose the marine ecosystem," he started. "Whales have blubber for different needs," he read. "It allows them to maintain their body heat and survive in very cold environments that would otherwise be uninhabitable to them, and some whales can also use their blubber for energy during times when food is scarce or during long trips. They eat zooplankton, krill, and copepods."

He pointed at the next picture and read, "Sharks have skin that's made up of a series of scales that act as an outer skeleton for easier movement and for saving energy. The upper side of a shark is commonly dark to blend in with water from above. The underside is white or lighter-coloured to blend in with the lighter surface of the sea from below. This camouflages them from predators and prey. They eat animals such as crustaceans, seas lions, and krill."

Gavin went on to talk about the other animals, and not once did he make eye contact with the class. It was part of the mark. But his presentation was going well. I liked how he designed his poster; the poster paper was blue like the ocean, and with a darker blue marker, he drew bubbles in different sizes. There were ten marine animals with information about them beside the picture it defined. He also had glittery ocean creature stickers scattered around.

There was only five minutes to the bell and Ms. Alcoser asked, "Who hasn't presented yet?"

Four people raised their hands.

"So you guys have to do it on Monday since you don't have this class on Friday."

"Your project looked really good," I commented to Gavin.

"Thanks. So did yours."

"Thank you."

The bell sounded and Gavin and I went to the cafeteria.

None of our friends were in sight, so we just sat at an empty table in front of each other. "I'm coming to watch you play," Gavin said.

"*Yay.*"

"Friday at seven, right?"

"Yep. I'm glad you're coming. I hope everyone else does, too."

He nodded.

"Hey." Max sat next to me.

"Hi," mine and Gavin's voices overlapped.

"I'm coming to your show."

"Oh, sweet. That's two so far," I said.

"So, you're going?" Max asked Gavin.

"Yep." He bit into his chocolate muffin.

Daniel, Johnny, and Valerie joined us a few minutes later. "I'm watching you play," was the first thing Valerie said as she sat next to Gavin, diagonal to me.

"Same," Daniel said from beside her.

Johnny had to lean backwards to see me past Max. "I still don't know. I've been so busy, I forgot to ask."

I was discouraged but still hopeful. "If you can't make it, don't worry about it."

"I can film it and send it to you," Max offered.

"I would just prefer to see it for myself. But if I don't come, please do that."

That was heartwarming.

"Hopefully we can all be there," Max said, smiling at me and wrapping his arm around my shoulders.

I returned the smile. I love my friends so much.

# THURSDAY

*Dear Diary,*

*Uncle Joseph picked me up from school today and we're going to his place to build a  birdhouse. Though I remember not liking woodwork in school, I think I might like it with him. I'm sure it will be fun.*

Uncle Joseph pulled into the driveway of his and Auntie Rebecca's small, dark tan house with a huge rosebush outside the living room window.

"Okay," he said as he took the key out of the ignition and got out of the truck.

I followed him into the garage.

"So, how big do you want it to be?" he asked.

"Maybe five by seven by nine inches." I thought for a moment. "I think that's a good size for small birds."

"It is. Did your teacher tell you that?"

I nodded.

He pointed to the shelf at the other side of the garage, storing different sizes of wood. "See the large, square pieces of wood at the bottom? Go get one. Be careful to not get splinters."

I went to the shelf and carefully dragged one out. It was quite hefty and I speed-walked with it to the table my uncle was putting a pencil and ruler on. He saw I couldn't handle it that well and put the piece of wood on the table for me. My arms felt light like cotton balls.

Uncle Joseph measured five inches in length. "Mark it there."

With a pencil, I made a small mark by his thumb. Then he measured the width. "And there."

I made another mark.

He took the pencil from my hand and drew a straight line from the marks to the edge of the wood, making a rectangle. He used a table saw to saw the rectangle out. Then we measured two identical rectangles that were seven inches in length and nine inches in height, another pair that were five inches in length and nine in height, and two smaller ones to be the pitched roof, and Uncle Joseph sawed them out. In one of the rectangles, he made a hole for birds to go through.

We began constructing the birdhouse with wood glue and nails.

We worked on it for a few hours, and like I expected, we stopped when it was almost halfway done.

"We'll have to finish it on Saturday and possibly Sunday," my uncle said.

"Hannah?"

We both turned to Auntie Rebecca in the doorway. "Would you like to stay for dinner?"

I waited a few seconds before replying with, "Okay."

"I'll tell your mom."

Thirty or so minutes later, dinner was ready and we sat at the kitchen table. On my plate were three tacos, fries, and ketchup.

We all ate in silence until my aunt asked, "How's the birdhouse coming along?"

Peering at her over my glass of Sprite, I said, "Good," and sipped my pop.

"I told her we can finish it on Saturday or Sunday," Uncle Joseph added.

"Oh, of course. Woodwork is time-consuming."

My uncle turned to me. "Were you having fun?"

"Yeah, I was," I said cheerfully.

"After dinner, would you like to see the dress I made earlier today?" Auntie Rebecca asked me.

"Sure." I'm always in the mood to see her hand-made clothing.

As Uncle Joseph did the dishes (after playfully bickering about whose turn it was), Auntie Rebecca led me upstairs to her bedroom. I leaned against the doorframe as she opened her closet and took out a dress on its hanger; the material was satin. The top was hot pink with short pale pink puffy sleeves and the ruffled skirt was also pale pink and was really long. There was thick black ribbon around the waist that twisted into a bow at the front. I adored it. "It's beautiful," I said admiringly. But I noticed it was way too small for her.

"I made it for you."

My heart jumped with happiness. "Really?" I gave her a big grin.

"Yeah. You can wear it tomorrow night. I'll step outside so you can put it on."

She gave it to me and I held it by the hanger. She shut the door and I gently laid it down on the bed and ran my hand over the dress's softness. I removed the hanger and put the dress on.

I stood before a tall mirror and admired what I saw, except my messy ponytail.

I pulled the elastic out and brushed my lion's mane with my fingers. When it became straighter, I put it in a ponytail and pulled it over my shoulder. Then I went back to studying my reflection.

I patted the puffy sleeves and touched the skirt that was so long it hid my feet. It was the most beautiful dress I've ever seen. I believe my aunt will be the fashion designer she's been dreaming of being. She's practically there.

I opened the door to reveal myself.

Auntie Rebecca's mouth fell open. "You're gorgeous!" she squealed.

"You did an amazing job," I complimented.

She put her hands to her mouth and became a tad bit teary. She was proud of her hard work. (Auntie Rebecca can be very emotional.)

"I'm going down for a nap…" Uncle Joseph stared at me… "now."

I smiled, proud to be wearing the most beautiful dress made by the world's greatest designer.

"You look lovely," my uncle said, eyeing me up and down.

"Thanks."

Auntie Rebecca shoved me gently back into her room. She opened her jewelry box and lifted a gold chain and put it on around my neck.

She placed me back in front of the mirror and stood behind me with her arms around my stomach and chin on my shoulder. "What do you think?"

I smiled again. "I love it."

# FRIDAY

*Dear Diary,*

*This is it. I'm going to perform on the stage for real again. Hopefully it won't be another disaster. I'm wearing the dress Auntie Rebecca made for me, plus the chain she lent me. I'm disappointed though. Johnny won't be coming, but he and Max agreed that Max will film me and send it to him. This time I want it to go right, and since I'm not being bullied anymore, I think it will.*

Just like the first time, my heart hammered anxiously. I was petrified and excited all over again.

After finding a stall in the overcrowded parking lot, my parents and I made our way into the theatre, the bottom of the skirt of my dressing brushing the ground. My friends, Auntie Rebecca, and Uncle Joseph were waiting in the lobby this time, surrounded by tons of people. And they stared at me in awe as I approached. "You're beautiful!" Valerie exclaimed.

I smiled and looked down at my dress. "Thanks. Auntie Rebecca made it."

My friends looked at my aunt in shock. "You made that?" they asked.

My aunt smiled proudly. "Yes."

"Wow!" Daniel exclaimed, examining my dress again. "Good job!"

"Thank you."

Just then, Gina came up to our group. "Hey, Hannah, are you...?" she studied me head to toe (though she couldn't see my toes)... "You look pretty."

I loved the compliments I was receiving. "Thank you."

She reached out her hand for mine and I reached for hers. Together, we made our way backstage where the other pianists were and everyone else went to sit.

Gina announced, "The show begins in five minutes," and everyone whirled to us and their eyes got stuck on my dress.

I liked the attention I was getting. It was building my confidence.

The other pianists dressed nice as well, like before. Sarah wore a pale orange dress that reached her knees. "Nice dress," she said.

"Thanks. Your dress is nice, too."

"Thank you."

As she was talking with her friend, I looked at her a little more; a pale orange dress that reached her knees and long sleeves with a swirly pattern, fancy white shoes with a bit of a heal, a long necklace with an amethyst charm, and a long blond braid.

It was time for the show to begin. The dark blue curtains spread apart and the spotlight shined down on the grand piano waiting to be played.

The audience erupted with applause.

The first pianist to go was one of the two boys. He walked onto the stage and sat before the piano, wearing a white and grey suit.

When everything was soundless, he began playing, filling the entire room with fast-paced music.

One by one, the pianists had their turn.

And then it was mine.

I settled my fear down as it arose increasingly. But when I raised my hands over the keys, I felt absolutely nothing. I took a breath so deep, it hurt my lungs. And I played.

When I finished, I had no memory of walking onstage and sitting down to play. It all went by so fast. But I knew I did a job well done.

The sound of erupting clapping and whistling filled my head with joy and pride. I've waited a long time for this. I faced the audience. At the back, I could see my family and friends. Well, most of them. Max's phone concealed his face.

I walked offstage. The pianists said things like, "good job," "you were excellent," and "you did great."

After ten minutes, I reunited with my friends and family in the packed lobby and I passed hugs around.

After giving Max a quick hug, he handed me his phone. "Johnny wants to talk to you."

I texted *Hey, it's Hannah.*

Then Johnny replied *Hey, you were amazing, I wish I could be there with you guys.*

*Yeah, we all wish you were, but there will be other times.*

*Hopefully I can be there next time.*

I sent a happy face emoji and gave Max his phone back.

We all chatted away until I felt some random urge to turn around to the window walls. I obeyed the urge and through the window was *them.* But they didn't have nasty glares like they usually did; they looked back at me with slight smiles.

I turned back to everyone else who were lost in two separate conversations.

And I still don't know why, but my feet led me away from them and out the doors to the former bullies. What was I thinking?

Outside, I faced *them.* Did the urge bring me here for a reason?

"We watched you," Piper said. "You were really good."

*What is this?* I thought.

"Um... thank you?"

"And your dress is very cool," Hope added.

I smiled. *Should I be careful not to fall for this?*

"Well done, Hannah." Ben walked passed the girls toward me and fist-bumped me.

*He actually said my name right.*

I thought it was so strange to be having a pleasant conversation with the five people who picked on me for so long.

"How did you know about the show?" I asked out of curiosity.

"I saw the email Gina sent out to everyone about it. Even though she's not my teacher anymore, I still got it," Hope said.

"We have to go," Willa said suddenly, looking down at her watch.

"It was nice talking to you," Piper said sweetly. And she led her brother and friends away, but as Willa and Stephanie passed, they said bye and to have a good weekend.

As they got tinier and tinier, I was in total shock. I was *not* expecting that.

I gazed up at the sky, the sun beginning to descend and I got lost in thought. I had a great performance, which I don't quite remember, and I possible befriended Piper, Stephanie, Willa, Ben, and Hope. I didn't know for sure if I formed five friendships. It didn't make sense I would. Not with them. But I figured that enemies can become friends.

I was so glad; the moment I waited for had finally arrived. I made myself and everyone who believed in me proud. But I have to give Mom and Max most of the credit; they helped me get here when I was afraid to.

I'm Hannah Little, and that was the story about my stage fright. (Plus everything else that was happening during that time.)